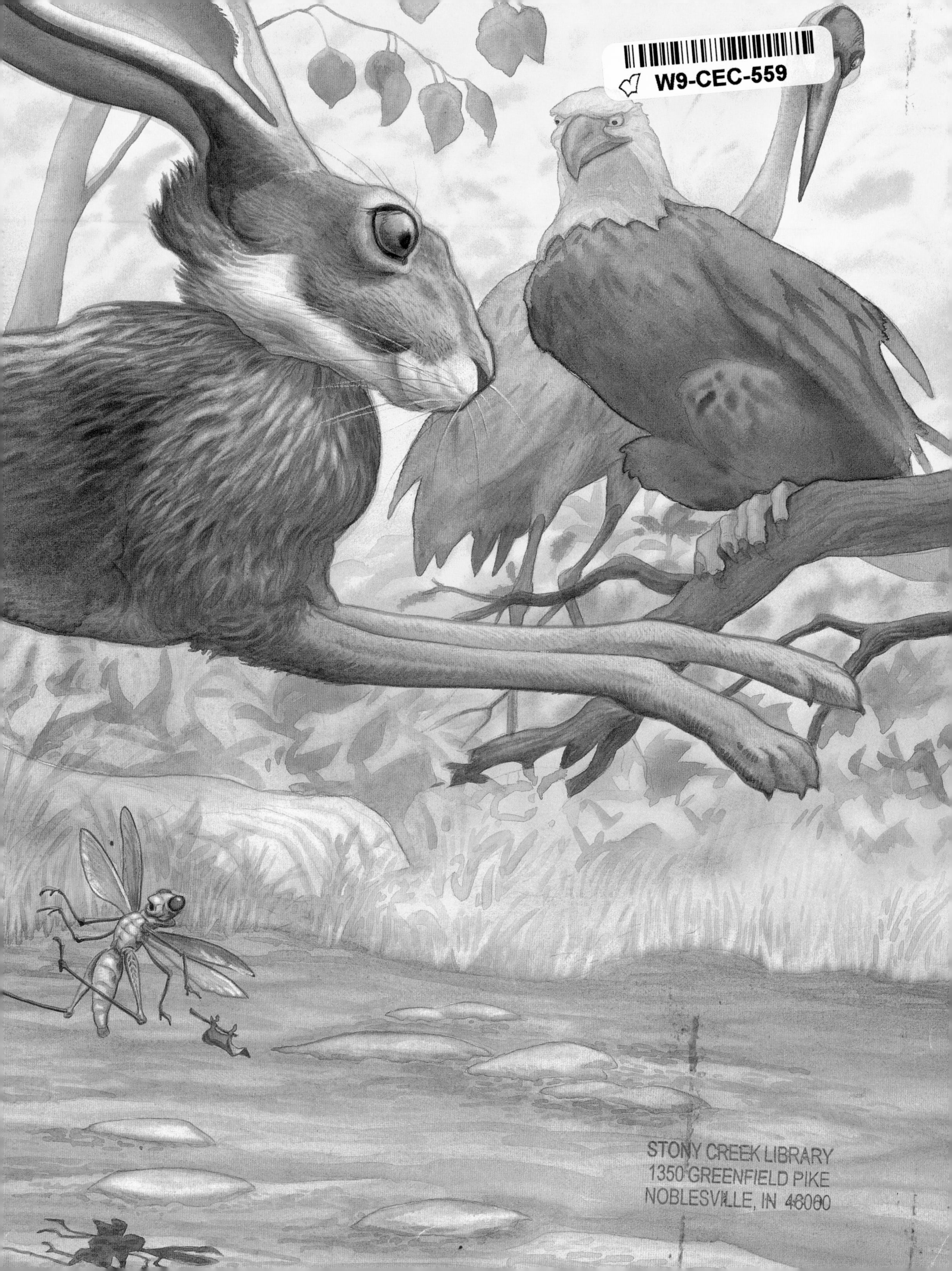

AESOP'S FABLES

Retold and illustrated by

Brad Sneed

Dial Books for Young Readers ▲ New York

For Steve

Published by Dial Books for Young Readers
A division of Penguin Young Readers Group
345 Hudson Street
New York, New York 10014

Copyright © 2003 by Bradley D. Sneed
Designed by Nancy R. Leo-Kelly
Text set in Berthold Baskerville
Manufactured in China on acid-free paper
1 3 5 7 9 10 8 6 4 2

Library of Congress Cataloging-in-Publication Data
Sneed, Brad.
Aesop's fables / retold and illustrated by Brad Sneed.
p.   cm.
Summary: Retellings of fifteen fables from Aesop, including, among
others, "The Stag at the Pool," "The Lion and the Mouse," and "The Vain Jackdaw."
ISBN 0-8037-2751-8
1. Aesop's fables—Adaptations. [1. Fables. 2. Folklore.] I. Aesop. II. Title.
PZ8.2.S56 Ae 2003   398.2 4'52—dc21   2002009470

The artwork for this book was created with watercolor, colored pencil, and acrylic on watercolor paper.

Contents

The Tortoise and the Eagle

"You flyers have all the fun." A tortoise lay in the dirt whining to the birds soaring overhead. "It's just not fair. You float with the clouds—I scrape over the rocks. You have the wind in your feathers—I have dust in my nose. Oh, won't any of you teach me to fly?"

An eagle was hovering nearby. "What's in it for me if I teach you to fly?"

"I'm rich," said the tortoise. "I'll trade half my gold for flying lessons."

"Prepare for takeoff," said the eagle as he hooked his talons to the tortoise's shell and pumped his wings. The eagle lifted the tortoise up, up, up above the clouds, and promptly let go.

The tortoise closed her eyes. The wind whistled in her ears. "I'm flying!" she yelled.

"We call that falling," answered the eagle.

The tortoise opened her eyes and saw jagged rocks below. "Landing lessons . . . I'll trade the rest of my gold for landing lessons!"

BE CAREFUL WHAT YOU WISH FOR.

The Fighting Roosters
and the Eagle

Two roosters battled in the barnyard. They kicked and slashed, gouged and pecked in a flurry of feathers and dust until one, bruised and battered, cried uncle and slunk off to a quiet corner. The other flapped to the top of a high wall to declare his triumph and claim the prize, KING OF THE FARMYARD! He crowed at the top of his lungs, so all would hear: "Behold your new king, the undisputed champ of the yard!" He strutted the entire length of the wall, bobbing his head and puffing his plumes. "I am the greatest fighter ever to grace this here chicken run! I am fast, strong, smart, and good-looking! Anybody wants to say different, step up now and prepare for a whuppin'! What?! Nobody wants a piece of me?"

"I'll take a piece." An eagle soaring high above noticed the spectacle below and sailed down to pluck the cocky bird off the wall. "Nothing I like better than a juicy piece of chicken!"

The new king stepped out of the corner and quietly watched the eagle fly away with lunch clutched in his talons.

PRIDE GOES BEFORE A FALL.

The Fox, the Rooster, and the Dog

One night a hungry fox was prowling around a farm. In the moonlight he saw a fat rooster snoozing on a high ledge. "Good news, good news!" he barked loud enough to wake the rooster.

"What, why, who, what news?" stammered the sleepy bird.

"King Lion has issued a proclamation!" said the wily fox. "There is to be a truce among the animals. No creature may harm another. We are all family and must live together in harmony. Come on down and give me a hug, brother rooster!"

"Glory be, that is wonderful news!" crowed the rooster. "And what good timing—look, the farmer's dog is coming over the hill. We three can party together!" The fox turned quickly to leave. "Mr. Fox, where are you going? Won't you stay and greet Mr. Dog on this happy occasion?"

"I would, to be sure," said the fox over his shoulder, "but I'm afraid Mr. Dog may not have heard King Lion's command."

CUNNING OFTEN OUTWITS ITSELF.

Belling the Cat

veryone knows that cats and mice are enemies, but what you may not know is long ago the mice gathered to discuss how to outsmart their crafty foe, the cat. One young mouse stood and addressed the crowd. "I think we can all agree that Mr. Cat is a sneak! He creeps close on padded paws, then silently strikes. How many of our kind—rest their souls—have had their lights snuffed without the slightest inkling that danger was a whisker away? I propose, therefore, that we acquire a small bell and attach it to the wretched beast. Then whenever we hear tinkling, we know to lay low."

The suggestion was met with wild applause and whistles and hoots of approval from the crowd of mice until one very old and well-respected mouse stood and raised his arm. "Very well," he said. "Who among us will bell the cat . . . any volunteers?"

All heads turned to the young mouse, who quietly lowered his eyes and sat on his hands.

IT IS EASY TO PROPOSE IMPOSSIBLE REMEDIES.

The Fox and the Crow

A crow flapped to a tree, where she prepared to munch on a hunk of cheese she had found, when she was interrupted by a voice from below.

"Hey, good-lookin', what's a beautiful chick like you doing in a dangerous forest like this?"

The startled crow looked down to see a fox sitting under her branch. She wanted to say, "I'm a crow, not a chicken!" But she had a beakful of cheese, so she merely blushed and cocked her head the way crows do.

The fox's eyes gleamed. He had a plan to get that cheese. "No, I mean it, you are a raving beauty!"

The crow wanted to say, "I'm a crow, not a raven, you silly." But as I said before, she was holding cheese in her mouth. So she giggled and turned away. (Being a crow, she wasn't used to someone going on about her looks.)

"Honestly"–the fox really turned on the charm now–"the sparkle in your eyes, the ruffle of your feathers . . . I mean . . . WOW! That pretty much says it–WOW! If only . . ."

The crow blinked and raised an eyebrow, waiting for the fox to go on.

"If only," the fox continued, "you had a voice as glorious as your looks, then you would without a doubt be Queen of the Birds."

The crow, forgetting for a moment that she was in fact a crow, opened her beak expecting to sing like a nightingale. What came out was a loud *CAW* and, more important, the piece of cheese, which bounced once and came to rest at the fox's feet. The fox trotted away, tail swinging. He would have said, "My dear Miss Crow, you have a voice, all right, but not much of a brain!" But he had a mouthful of cheese!

FLATTERERS ARE NOT TO BE TRUSTED.

The Crow and the Pitcher

"Golly, I'm parched." A crow was flying over a dry, barren land. "I'm doomed if I don't find water soon!" Then, as fate would have it, she spied a pitcher, of all things, sitting among a pile of rocks and pebbles. "Please, please, please, let there be water," she pleaded. The crow perched on the pitcher and peeked in. Sure enough, it contained water. "Hallelujah," she exclaimed, and thrust her head in, anxious for a taste. But confound it, the pitcher's neck was so long and narrow, she couldn't reach the liquid.

Desperate for a drink, she tried to tip the pitcher. She leaned against it and pushed. It didn't budge. She kicked it. It didn't move. She picked up a pebble and pecked at the pitcher. Its clay walls were thick. It didn't crack.

The clever crow didn't give up. She hopped to the pitcher top and dropped in the pebble. *Bloop*. She added another. *Blop*. She picked up more pebbles and dropped them one by one into the pitcher. *Plink, plunk, plop*. Each pebble the crow added raised the water level in the pitcher. After many pebbles, at last she dipped her dusty beak and took a long drink.

NECESSITY IS THE MOTHER OF INVENTION.

The Town Mouse
and the Country Mouse

A Country Mouse and her Town Mouse guest sat down to dinner at the edge of a plowed field. The Country Mouse gnawed on a wheat seed. "Dig in," she insisted, offering her friend a clod-covered root.

The Town Mouse brushed dust from his whiskers and turned up his nose. "Excuse me, cousin, but this is ant food. Let's blow this hayseed stand and get a real meal." He grabbed his friend's hand. "To town, and a taste of the sweet life!"

After a long walk, the pair finally skinnied under Town Mouse's back door. They crept down a dark hall to a grand dining room and shimmied to the top of a grand table, where the remains of a grand feast lay before them. "Behold," said Town Mouse, arms outstretched.

"Mother of plenty," exclaimed Country Mouse, swallowing hard. Loud barking interrupted their sprint for the chocolate cake. "What's that?" hissed Country Mouse.

"Only the dogs of the house," replied Town Mouse.

"Only!" cried Country Mouse. "Good-bye, cousin."

"What, leaving so soon?" asked the other.

"Yes," she replied. "Why munch on cake, only to become a dog's dessert?"

BETTER TO MUNCH ON GRAIN IN SAFETY THAN TO NIBBLE ON CAKE IN FEAR.

The Lion and the Mouse

A mouse skittered across a sleeping lion's nose. Before you could say "twitching whisker"–CLUMP!–the lion covered the mouse with his paw. "You tickled my nose, you measly mouse. I think now you will tickle inside my tummy!"

The mouse peeked between the lion's claws. "Your Majesty, before you swallow me, consider this: If you let me go, I will never forget it. Perhaps one day I shall return the favor and save your life."

At this, the lion roared with laughter. "It would be a shame to eat such a witty little creature. Run free, funny fellow. I will sleep well tonight knowing you are watching over me." The lion's loud laughter shook the ground beneath the mouse's feet as he scampered away.

Later, the mouse heard a familiar roar; not a roar of laughter, but a desperate roar for help. He ran to the lion, who was tangled in a hunter's net. The mouse quickly chewed through the cords with his small sharp teeth, freeing the lion. "It is pretty funny, Your Majesty," chuckled the mouse, "to think that a tiny mouse could save the King of the Beasts!"

NO ACT OF MERCY, HOWEVER SMALL, IS EVER WASTED.

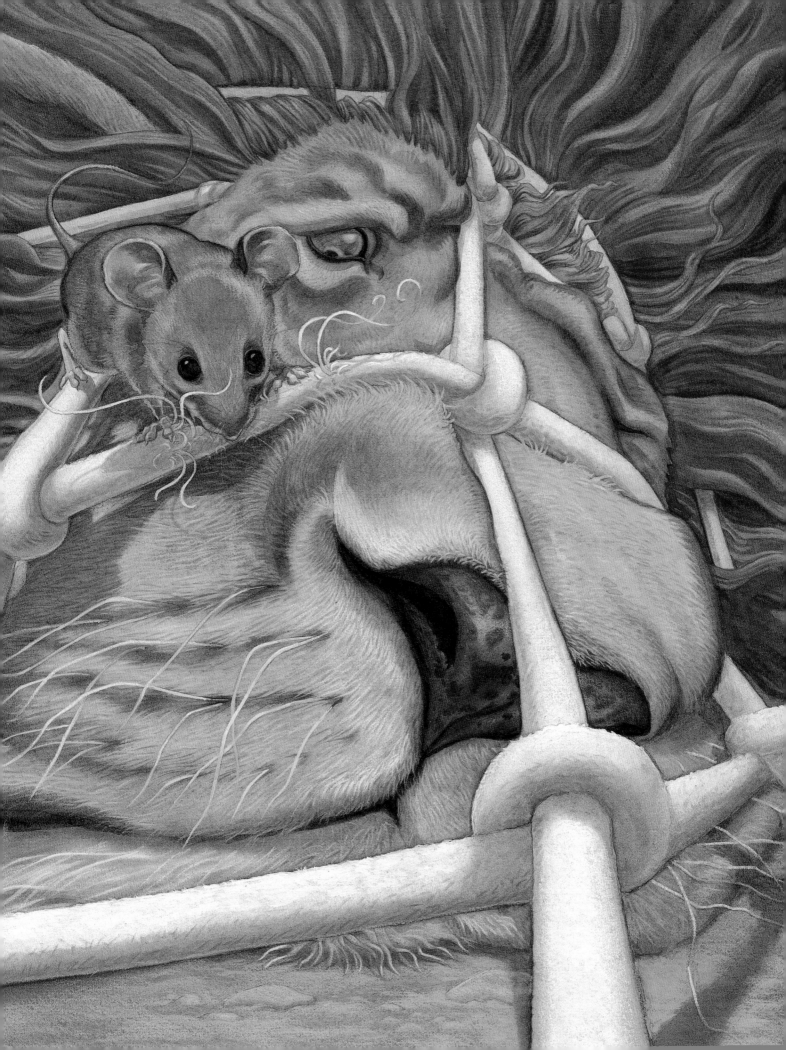

The Caged Bird
and the Bat

A small cage hung outside a window. Confined within the bars was a beautiful little songbird. The bird had a beautiful singing voice. *"Twitter-tweet, tootle doodle, twitter-tweet."* The sweet notes drifted softly into the darkness, for it was still night. When the sun began to peek over the distant rooftops, a strange thing happened—the bird fell silent.

A bat, thinking this odd behavior for a bird, winged over and hung bat-style from the cage bars. "Excuse me, sir, I don't mean to be rude, but why do you sing when other birds sleep?"

"Ah, I have a very good reason," whispered the bird. "One bright day when I was singing from the branches, a bird catcher followed the sound of my voice and cast his net over me. Now I sing only under the cover of darkness."

"A good strategy," said the smirking bat, "for a bird that flies free!"

AN OUNCE OF PREVENTION IS WORTH A POUND OF CURE.

The Vain Jackdaw

"Listen up, everyone, this is Jupiter, Supreme Being, Head Honcho, Ruler of All Things. I have an important announcement for my fine feathered citizens. Tomorrow, at my place, there will be a pageant where I, as judge, will select the most spectacular among you to be King of All Birds."

Upon hearing this news, the birds flocked to the community pool to bathe and preen their feathers, for they all wanted to look their best at the competition. The plain jackdaw was there with the rest, and realized that with his ugly plumage he didn't have a prayer of capturing old Jupiter's attention, so he waited for the other birds to finish primping and go home to get their beauty rest. He then waded about collecting the most brilliant, fancy feathers the others had dropped, and fastened the plumes to his own drab body.

The following day each bird strutted before Jupiter's throne. After careful consideration, Jupiter was about to appoint the jackdaw king, when the other contestants recognized the imposter and plucked the false feathers, exposing him as the ordinary jackdaw.

THOSE WHO CHEAT LOSE IN THE END.

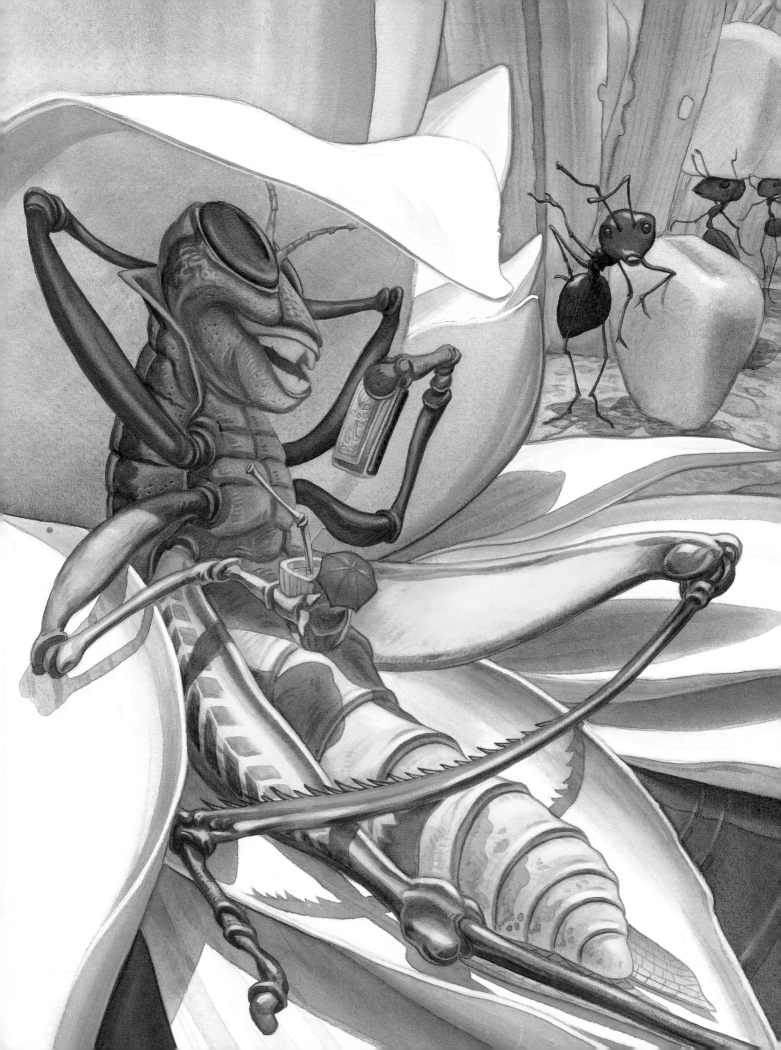

The Ant and the Grasshopper

While lounging on a floating lily a carefree grasshopper puffed on a tiny harmonica. After playing a jaunty tune, he hollered to a colony of bustling ants as they filed by. "Fellas, fellas, slow down. You're working way too hard." Each ant toiled with a grain he carried from a nearby field to an underground storage room. "Come on, guys, it's a beautiful summer afternoon. Take a load off. Come dangle your busy little tootsies in the pool—or better yet, grab a partner and sashay on over. I'm just getting warmed up! Besides, all your marching is messing up my rhythm!"

One serious little ant stepped out of line. "We are gathering food for winter, sir, and if you don't mind a little friendly advice, I suggest you do the same." And without another word he balanced a kernel of corn on his head and shuffled back to the procession.

The grasshopper scoffed, "The sun is warm, the water cool, my belly is full. I think I'll take a little nap. You boys have a nice day." He sipped his drink and sang himself to sleep.

A few months later, the starving grasshopper trudged through deep snow to the anthill and begged for a morsel of food. He recognized the ant that spoke to him by the pool. "Mr. Grasshopper, I can see you've changed your tune. A fool who sings away the summer, dances a hungry jig in winter."

IT IS BEST TO FINISH YOUR CHORES BEFORE YOU PLAY.

The Wolf and the Crane

A crane was fishing in the marsh when a sickly-looking wolf stumbled over. The crane noticed right away the wolf wasn't well. He had a runny nose, and sticky strings of saliva hung from droopy jowls. Before the bird could back away (she was recovering from a cold herself and didn't want to catch the wolf's illness) the wolf sputtered, gagged, sniffed, gurgled, gulped, and hacked up a hoarse, rasping, froth-spraying cough. The disgusted crane dipped her head in the water, washing wolf spittle from her feathers.

"Well, I never . . . Do you mind?! I am sorry you're sick, but you are infecting the entire forest with your germs! Didn't your mother teach you to cover your mouth?"

"You don't understand," rattled the wolf. "I'm not ill. I have a bone stuck in my throat. I came over to ask if you would kindly remove it." The wolf gagged and hacked again, spitting on the ground.

"It stands to reason, I suppose, that an ill-mannered animal such as your-self would not chew his food properly," said the indignant crane. "Perhaps that bone should remain lodged in your gullet as a painful reminder not to wolf down your supper."

"Oh, have pity," pleaded the wolf. "I can offer you a reward."

"In that case," said the crane, "let's have a look. Say *Ahhhhhh*." The crane's tweezer-like beak was perfectly suited for the task. In no time she plucked the sharp bone from the wolf's throat. Without a word of thanks, the wolf turned and loped away.

"Hey, what about my reward?" called the crane.

The wolf spun and sprinted back to the startled crane. He sneered and clicked his razor-sharp teeth. "You placed your head in a wolf's mouth and lived to tell about it. What more could you ask for? Now fly, fly away, Miss Birdie, or I will eat you for dessert." Then he leaned close and whispered, "I promise to chew every bite forty times!"

THOSE WHO EXPECT THANKS FROM RASCALS ARE OFTEN DISAPPOINTED.

The Stag at the Pool

A thirsty stag came to a clear pool for a drink of water. He saw his reflection and paused to admire his magnificent antlers. "Lucky me. I must have the largest and most shapely rack of any deer on the plain," he thought. "But gracious, look at my legs." His legs were long and lean. "How awfully embarrassing," he snorted. "If only my puny legs were as grand as my antlers."

The stag didn't notice that a lion crouched in the tall grass nearby. The lion didn't care about the stag's antlers or his skinny legs. She licked her lips and thought how yummy fresh venison would taste this morning. When she sprang from her hiding place, the startled stag darted away. The chase was on. The lion was fast, but on the flat, open plain she couldn't overtake the stag. On long, nimble legs, the stag bounded far out ahead of the pursuing lion.

When the stag turned into the woods, his massive antlers knocked against low branches and became entangled in a snarl of vines and underbrush. He tried desperately to free himself but it was no use; the lion would have venison steak for breakfast after all.

"What an idiot I am," said the stag. "I despise these legs, yet they would have saved my life if my beloved antlers hadn't gotten in the way!"

WE DO NOT OFTEN APPRECIATE THE PLAIN AND PRACTICAL.

The Ox and the Frog

Nearly breathless and waving his arms wildly, a very young frog bounded up to his dozing father. "Holy cow! Pop . . . Pop, you won't believe it . . . an incredible sight . . . a creature . . . a monster . . . a stupendous, gargantuan mountain of a beast with terrible horns that brush the clouds and a body so wide it blocks the sun . . . holy cow!"

The old frog rolled his eyes. "Oh pooh, son, what you saw was not a terrible beast at all, but merely Farmer White's lazy ox. I know for a fact that animal is not much taller than I am, and I can easily make myself as wide. Stand back, son, and watch your old dad." Father frog sucked in air and held his breath, blowing himself up like a shiny green balloon. "Was the ox as big as this?"

"Oh, much bigger than that, Pop!"

The old frog gulped more air and puffed harder. "As big as this?"

"Much, much bigger!"

Father frog, determined not to be overshadowed by a silly ox, sucked and puffed, gulped and gasped, huffed and poofed until he was so swollen and round that he nearly rolled from his mud nest into the nearby pond. "Now, son," he said with some difficulty, "that . . . ox . . . couldn't . . . be . . . as . . . big . . . as . . ." KER-BLAM!

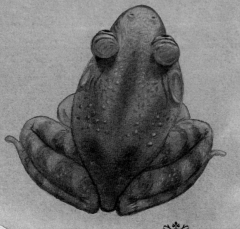

A BIG HEAD MAY LEAD TO ONE'S OWN UNDOING.

The Gnat and the Bull

A gnat settled on a bull's horn to rest. He sat, and sat, and sat, and sat. Then he adjusted himself and sat some more. When he was finally ready to fly on, he buzzed, "Mr. Bull, would you like me to leave you alone?"

The bull grunted, "Oh, Mr. Gnat, I didn't realize you were up there, so I suppose I won't miss you when you're gone."

WE ARE NOT ALWAYS AS IMPORTANT AS WE THINK WE ARE.